To N.C.,
For all your help,

B. R.

1980 PRINTING

Copyright © 1978 by Platt & Munk, Publishers
All rights reserved under International and
Pan-American Copyright Conventions.
Printed in the United States of America
Library of Congress Catalog Card Number: 77-90512

ISBN: 0-448-47613-4 (Trade Edition)
ISBN: 0-448-13028-9 (Library Edition)

Designed by Natalie Provenzano, A Good Thing, Inc.

The Animal Storybook

Illustrated by Robert Frank
Edited by Beverly Reingold

Platt & Munk/New York
A Division of Grosset & Dunlap

Why the Bear has a Stumpy Tail

Long ago, on a silver day in winter, the Bear was out walking in the forest, when he met the Fox slinking along with a string of stolen fish in his jaws.

"Where did you get those?" he asked, for the Bear doted on fish, but could rarely catch any himself.

"I cannot tell a lie," said the Fox, turning up his eyes in an innocent manner. "I got them by fishing."

"I wish I could fish half so well," said the Bear. "Is there a trick to it?"

"For a creature of your intelligence," said the Fox, "it is the easiest thing in the world. You need only stroll out on the ice, cut a hole, and lower your tail down through. You may soon find your tail stings and smarts a little. But that's a good sign, for it shows the fish are biting. The longer you hold out, the more fish you will get. When you are certain you have plenty, pull out your tail like a true bear, with a strong pull sideways and all your weight to help you."

"It certainly sounds easy, the way you put it," agreed the Bear, and toddling off to the lake, he followed the Fox's instructions. He sat with his tail down through the ice so long that it became completely frozen. Thus when he pulled it out with a strong pull sideways and all his weight to help him, it snapped off. And that is why the bear walks the forest with a stumpy tail to this very day.

The Cheshire Cat
(From Alice's Adventures in Wonderland)

It was in the Duchess's kitchen that Alice first saw the Cheshire Cat. There it lay, grinning from ear to ear.

"I didn't know that Cheshire cats grinned," said Alice. "In fact, I didn't know that cats *could* grin."

"They all can," said the Duchess, "and most of 'em do."

Later—after the Duchess had thrown her baby into Alice's arms and run off to play croquet with the Queen; and after Alice had taken the baby outside; and after the baby had turned into a pig and trotted away squealing—Alice saw the Cheshire Cat again. It was sitting on a bough of a tree, just a

few yards from Alice. The Cat grinned when it saw her.

"Cheshire Puss," said Alice, "would you tell me, please, which way I ought to go from here?"

"That depends a good deal on where you want to get to," said the Cat.

"I don't much care where—" said Alice.

"Then it doesn't matter which way you go," said the Cat.

"So long as I get *somewhere*," Alice added as an explanation.

"Oh, you're sure to do that," said the Cat, "if only you walk long enough."

Alice felt this could not be denied, so she tried another question. "What sort of people live around here?"

"In *that* direction," the Cat said, waving its right paw, "lives the Hatter. And in *that* direction"—waving the other paw—"lives the March Hare. Visit either you like; they're both mad."

"But I don't want to go among mad people," Alice remarked.

"Oh, you can't help that," said the Cat. "We're all mad here. I'm mad. You're mad."

"How do you know I'm mad?" said Alice.

"You must be," said the Cat, "or you wouldn't have come here."

Alice didn't think that proved it at all. However, she went on. "And how do you know you're mad?"

"To begin with," said the Cat, "a dog's not mad. You grant that?"

"I suppose so," said Alice.

"Well," the Cat went on, "a dog growls when it's angry and wags its tail when it's pleased. I growl when I'm pleased and wag my tail when I'm angry. Therefore I'm mad."

"I call it purring, not growling," said Alice.

"Call it what you like," said the Cat. "Are you playing croquet with the Queen today?"

"I should like to very much," said Alice, "but I haven't been invited yet."

"You'll see me there," said the Cat, and vanished.

Alice was not much surprised at this, as she was getting so well used to queer things happening. That was a good thing, for while she was still looking at the place where it had been, the Cat suddenly appeared again.

"By the way, what became of the baby?" said the Cat. "I'd nearly forgotten to ask."

"It turned into a pig," Alice answered very quietly, just as if the Cat had come back in a natural way.

"I thought it would," said the Cat, and vanished again.

Alice waited a little, half expecting to see it again, but it did not appear. After a minute or two she walked on in the direction in which the March Hare was said to live. "I've seen hatters before," she said to herself. "The March Hare will be the more interesting, and perhaps, as this is May, it won't be raving mad—at least not so mad as it was in March." As she said this, she looked up. There was the Cat again, sitting on a branch of a tree.

"Did you say *pig*, or *fig*?" said the Cat.

"I said *pig*," replied Alice. "And I wish you wouldn't keep appearing and vanishing so suddenly. You make one quite giddy!"

"All right," said the Cat, and this time it vanished very slowly, beginning with the end of the tail, and ending with the grin, which remained some time after the rest of it had gone.

"Well!" thought Alice. "I've often seen a cat without a grin, but a grin without a cat! It's the most curious thing I ever saw in all my life!"

Bear and Fox in Partnership

The Great Red Fox wished to go into partnership with Uncle Bear. Now, Uncle Bear had a pot of honey and a big cheese to share, but the Great Red Fox had only his wits. Wits, we know, cannot be shared in partnership like a pot of honey and a big cheese. But when the Great Red Fox said to Uncle Bear, "A head full of wits is worth more than a pot of honey and a big cheese," Uncle Bear agreed to the partnership.

The pot of honey and the big cheese were stored away for a rainy day. It had been decided that only the wits would be used

at the moment. "Very well," thought the fox. "I'll just rattle them up a bit and see what happens."

Shortly, the Great Red Fox turned to Uncle Bear and said, "I am sick today and must go see Master Doctor." And then off he went—but not to the doctor. No, indeed! The Great Red Fox marched straight to the storehouse and ate part of the honey. Then he lay out in the sun and toasted his skin until he was quite ready to go home again.

"Well," said Uncle Bear when the fox walked in, "how do you feel now?"

"Oh, quite well," said the Great Red Fox.

"And was the medicine bitter?" said Uncle Bear.

"Oh, no, it was good enough," said the Great Red Fox.

"And how much did the doctor give you?" said Uncle Bear.

"Oh, one part of a pot full," said the Great Red Fox.

"My goodness," thought Uncle Bear, "that is a great deal of medicine to take."

Things went smoothly until the fox grew hungry for another taste of honey. This time he said he had to go see his aunt. And off he went to the storehouse, where he ate all the honey he wanted. Then, after he had slept a bit in the sun, he went home.

"Well," said Uncle Bear, "did you see your aunt?"

"Oh, yes," said the Great Red Fox.

"And did she give you anything?" said Uncle Bear.

"Oh, yes," said the Great Red Fox.

"And what was it she gave you?" said Uncle Bear.

"Why, she gave me another part of a pot full," said the Great Red Fox.

"How nice," said Uncle Bear, thinking what a queer thing that was to give.

By and by, the Great Red Fox began thinking of honey again. He told Uncle Bear he had a christening to go to. Then off he went to the pot of honey, and this time he finished it all and licked the pot into the bargain.

"Did everything go smoothly at the christening?" said Uncle Bear.

"Oh, smoothly enough," said the Great Red Fox.

"And did they have a christening feast?" said Uncle Bear.

"Oh, yes," said the Great Red Fox.

"And what did they have?" said Uncle Bear.

"Oh, everything that was in the pot," said the Great Red Fox.

"Dear, dear," said Uncle Bear. "They must have been a hungry set at that christening."

One day not long afterward, Uncle Bear said, "Let us have a feast and eat up the pot of honey and the big cheese. We'll ask Father Goat over to help us."

That suited the Great Red Fox well enough. So while Uncle Bear went to invite Father Goat to the feast, the Great Red Fox ran to the storehouse to fetch the pot of honey and the big cheese.

"See, now," said the Great Red Fox to himself, "the pot of honey and the big cheese belong together, and it is a pity to part them." So without further ado, he sat down and ate the entire cheese.

When he went home again, the Great Red Fox found Father Goat toasting his toes at the fire and waiting for supper. Uncle Bear sat on the back doorstep sharpening the bread knife.

"Hello!" said the Great Red Fox. "And what are you doing here, Father Goat?"

"I am waiting for supper," said Father Goat.

"And where is Uncle Bear?" said the Great Red Fox.

"He is sharpening the bread knife," said Father Goat.

"Ah, yes," said the Great Red Fox. "And when he is through with that, he is going to cut off your tail."

Father Goat became instantly terrified. That house was no place for him, and that he could see with one eye shut. Off he marched as though the ground were hot under him.

The Great Red Fox went out to Uncle Bear. "That was a pretty body you asked to take supper with us," he said. "He has marched off with the pot of honey and the big cheese, leaving us to sit down and whistle over an empty table between us."

When Uncle Bear heard this, he did not tarry. Up he got and off he went after Father Goat. "Stop! Stop!" he bawled. "Let me have a little, at least."

But Father Goat thought that Uncle Bear was speaking of his tail, for he knew nothing of the pot of honey and the big cheese. So he just knuckled down to it and scampered away, the gravel flying behind him.

Now nothing was left to the partners but the wits the Great Red Fox had brought into the business. One day the Great Red Fox said to Uncle Bear, "I saw them shaking the apple trees at Farmer John's today. And if you've a mind to try the wits that belong to us, we'll go and get a bagful apiece from the storehouse at the farm."

Uncle Bear agreed. So off they marched, each with an empty bag, to fetch the apples. The door at the storehouse was not locked, so they walked right in and began filling their bags with apples. The Great Red Fox tumbled them into his bag as fast as he could, taking them just as they came, good or bad. But Uncle Bear took his time about it and picked the apples carefully, for he wanted the best that were to be had.

Naturally, the Great Red Fox had his bag full before Uncle

Bear had picked out half a score of good juicy apples. "I'll just peep out of the window," said the Great Red Fox, "and see if Farmer John is coming." But to himself he said, "I'll slip outside and turn the key of the door on Uncle Bear, for somebody will have to carry the blame for this, and his skin is tougher than mine. He will never be able to get out of that little window."

The Great Red Fox then jumped up to the window. But now the scales were tipping, for in the window a trap had been set to catch rats. And as the Great Red Fox leaped from the window, the trap caught him by the tail and left him hanging.

Soon Uncle Bear bawled, "Is Farmer John coming?"

"Hush! Hush!" said the Great Red Fox, trying to get his tail out of the trap.

"No, no," bawled Uncle Bear, louder than before. "Tell me if Farmer John is coming."

Yes, Farmer John was coming, for he had heard the hubbub, and here he was with five of his men and three great dogs. "Oh, Farmer John," said the Great Red Fox, "don't touch me. I am not the thief. Uncle Bear, in the pantry, is the one."

But Farmer John saw only that here was a rogue of a fox caught in the trap, and the farmer had a fine beating ready for him. When the Great Red Fox realized this, he pulled with all his might, breaking off his tail close to his body. Then away he ran, with Farmer John, the men, and the dogs close to his heels. But Uncle Bear filled his bag full of the choicest apples. And as the coast was clear, he walked quietly out of the door and went home.

Thus it was that Uncle Bear and the Great Red Fox formed a partnership, and each benefitted from what the other brought to it. And the only reason for that is that Justice intervened—as she sometimes does.

The Fox and the Grapes

A hungry Fox saw some fine bunches of grapes hanging from a vine that grew along a high trellis. He did his best to reach them by jumping as high as he could into the air. But it was all in vain, for they were just out of reach. So he gave up trying and walked away with an air of dignity and unconcern, remarking, "I thought those grapes were ripe, but now I see they are quite sour."

The Tortoise and the Hare

The Hare was always poking fun at the Tortoise for being so slow. One day the Tortoise surprised the Hare by saying, "I challenge you to a race." The Hare was much amused at the idea. "By all means," said he.

Both started off together. Before long the Hare was so far ahead that he thought he might as well have a rest. He lay down and soon fell fast asleep. The Tortoise, however, kept plodding on until he reached the goal. Finally the Hare awoke with a start and dashed on at his fastest—only to find that the Tortoise had already won the race.

The Lion and the Mouse

A Lion asleep in his lair was awakened by a Mouse running over his face. Losing his temper, he seized it with his paw. He was about to kill it, when the Mouse, terrified, begged him to spare its life. "Please let me go," it cried, "and someday I will repay you for your kindness." The idea of so weak a creature ever being able to do anything for him amused the Lion, and he good-humoredly let it go.

One day the Lion got entangled in a net which had been spread for game by some hunters. The Mouse heard his roars of anger and ran to the spot. Immediately, it began to gnaw the ropes with its teeth, and before long succeeded in setting the Lion free. "There!" said the Mouse. "You laughed when I promised to repay you, but now you see that a Mouse can indeed help a Lion."

The Stag at the Pool

A thirsty Stag went down to a pool to drink. As he bent over the surface, he saw his reflection in the water and was struck with admiration for his fine spreading antlers. At the same time, he felt nothing but disgust for the slenderness and weakness of his legs.

While he stood there looking at himself, he was seen and attacked by a Lion. In the chase which followed, the Stag soon drew away from his pursuer and kept his lead as long as the ground over which he ran was open and free of trees. But on entering a wood, he was caught by his antlers in the branches and fell a victim to the teeth and claws of his enemy. "Woe is me!" he cried with his last breath. "I despised my legs, which might have saved my life, but I gloried in my horns, and they have proved my ruin."

The Ass in the Lion's Skin

An Ass found a lion's skin and dressed himself up in it. Then he went about frightening everyone he met, for they all took him to be a lion and ran when they saw him coming. Elated by the success of his trick, he brayed loudly in triumph. The Fox heard him and, recognizing him at once for the Ass he was, said to him, "Oho, my friend, it's you, is it? I, too, should have been afraid if I hadn't heard your voice."

The Fox without a Tail

A Fox once fell into a trap. He managed to get free, but he lost his brush in the attempt. He was then so ashamed of his appearance that he thought life would not be worth living unless he could persuade the other foxes to part with their tails, also, thus diverting attention from his own loss.

He called a meeting of all the foxes and advised them to cut off their tails. "They're ugly things," he said. "And besides, they're heavy, and it's tiresome to be always carrying them about with you." But one of the other foxes said, "My friend, if you hadn't lost your own tail, you wouldn't be so keen on getting us to cut off ours."

Puss in Boots

Once there was a miller whose sole worldly possessions were his mill, his ass, and his cat. That was all he had to leave his three sons upon his death. So he called in no lawyer and made no will, but simply left the mill to the eldest, the ass to the second, and the cat to the youngest.

The youngest son was quite downcast about his inheritance. "My brothers," he said to himself, "by putting their goods together will be able to earn an honest livelihood. But once I have eaten my cat and sold his skin, I shall have nothing."

Puss, who was sitting quietly on the window seat, overheard these words. Looking up, he said with a very serious, sober air, "Please, dear master, do not worry about your future. Only give me a bag and a pair of boots, so that I may stride through the brambles, and you will soon see that you have a better bargain than you think."

As soon as Puss was provided with what he had asked for, he drew on his boots and, slinging the bag round his neck, took hold of the two strings with his forepaws. Then he set off for a warren he knew was stocked with rabbits. There he filled his bag with bran and weeds, stretched himself out as stiffly as though he were dead, and waited patiently till some simple young rabbit, unused to worldly snares and wiles, should see the dainty feast. He had lain scarcely a few moments, before a thoughtless young rabbit caught at the bait and went headlong into the bag. Immediately, the cat drew the strings and strangled the foolish creature.

Puss was vastly proud of his victory. He went straight to the palace to see the king. When he was shown into the king's cabinet, he bowed respectfully to His Majesty and said, "Sire, I bring you a rabbit from the warren of the Marquis of Carabas." (Such was the title the cat took it into his head to give his master.)

"Tell your master that I am obliged by his courtesy, and that I accept his present with much pleasure," replied the king.

Later Puss went and hid himself in a cornfield, and held his bag open as before. Soon two partridges were lured into the trap. Puss quickly drew the strings and made them both prisoners. He then went and presented them to the king, as he had done the rabbit. The king received the partridges very graciously, and ordered the messenger to be rewarded for his trouble. For two or three months, Puss continued to carry game to the king, always presenting it in the name of his master, the Marquis of Carabas.

One day Puss happened to hear that the king was going to take a drive along the bank of the river, accompanied by his daughter, the most beautiful princess in the world. He said to his master, "If you follow my advice, your fortune will be as good as made. You need only go and bathe in the river at the spot that I shall point out, and leave the rest to me."

The marquis did as his cat advised. As he was bathing, the king came driving past. Puss began to bawl as loudly as he could, "Help! Help! The Marquis of Carabas is drowning!"

On hearing this, the king looked out of the carriage window. Recognizing the cat who had so often brought him game, he ordered his bodyguard to fly to the assistance of the Marquis of Carabas.

While the poor marquis was being fished out of the river,

Puss stepped up to the royal carriage. He told His Majesty that during the time his master was bathing, some robbers had stolen his clothes. Puss, of course, had hidden them under a large stone. The king immediately ordered the gentlemen of his wardrobe to go and fetch one of his most sumptuous dresses for the Marquis of Carabas.

When the marquis, who was a handsome young fellow, came forth gaily dressed, he looked so elegant that the king took him for a very fine gentleman, and the princess fell head over heels in love with him. The king insisted on his getting into the carriage and taking a drive with them.

Puss, highly delighted at the turn things were taking, and determined that all should turn out in the very best way, now ran on before the carriage. When he reached a meadow where some peasants were mowing the grass, he hurried up to them. "I say, good folk," he cried, "if you do not tell the king, when he comes this way, that the field you are mowing belongs to the Marquis of Carabas, you shall all be chopped to bits."

When the carriage passed by, the king put his head out and asked the mowers whose good grassland that was. "It belongs to the Marquis of Carabas, please Your Majesty," said they breathlessly, for the cat's threats had frightened them mightily.

"Upon my word, Marquis," said the king, "that is a fine estate you have."

"Yes, sire," replied the marquis with an easy air. "It yields me a tolerable income every year."

Puss, who continued to run on before the carriage, presently came up to some reapers. "I say, you reapers," cried he, "mind you tell the king that this corn belongs to the Marquis of Carabas, or else you shall all be chopped into mincemeat."

The king passed by a moment after and inquired to whom those cornfields belonged. "To the Marquis of Carabas, please

Your Majesty," replied the reapers.

"Faith, it pleases me right well to see the beloved marquis is so wealthy!" said the king.

Puss kept running on before the carriage and repeating the same instructions to all the laborers he met, and the king was astounded at the vast possessions of the Marquis of Carabas. He kept congratulating the marquis, while the newly-made nobleman received each fresh compliment more lightly than the last, so that one could see he really was a marquis, and a very grand one, too.

At length Puss reached a magnificent castle belonging to an ogre, who was immensely rich, since all the lands the king had been riding through were a portion of his estate. Puss inquired what sort of a person the ogre might be, and what he was able to do. Then he sent in a message asking leave to speak with the ogre, adding that he was unwilling to pass so near his castle without paying his respects to him.

The ogre received Puss as civilly as it is in the nature of an ogre to do. "I have been told," said Puss, "that you have the power of transforming yourself into all sorts of animals, such as a lion or an elephant."

"So I have," replied the ogre sharply. "Do you doubt it? Look, and you shall see me become a lion at once."

When Puss suddenly saw a lion before him, he was seized with such a fright that he scrambled up to the roof, although it was no easy job, owing to his boots. When the ogre had returned to his natural shape, Puss came down again and confessed he had been exceedingly frightened.

"I have also been told," added Puss, "only I really cannot believe it, that you likewise possess the power of taking the shape of the smallest animals, and that you could change yourself into a rat or a mouse. But that is surely impossible."

"Impossible, indeed!" cried the ogre. "You shall see."

So saying, the ogre took on the shape of a mouse, and began frisking about on the ground. Puss immediately pounced upon him, gave him one shake, and put an end to him.

By this time the king had reached the gates of the ogre's magnificent castle. Puss, hearing the rumbling of the carriage across the drawbridge, ran out to meet the king, crying, "Your Majesty is welcome to the castle of the Marquis of Carabas."

"What! My dear Marquis," exclaimed the king, "does this castle also belong to you? Really, I never saw anything more splendid than the courtyard and the surrounding buildings. Pray let us see if the inside is equal to the outside."

The marquis gracefully helped the princess out of the carriage. Following the king, they mounted a flight of steps and were ushered by Puss into a vast hall, where they found an elegant feast spread. Some of the ogre's friends were to have visited him that day, but the news had spread that the king was about, and they dared not come.

The king was positively delighted. The castle was magnificent, and the Marquis of Carabas was such an excellent young man. Furthermore, the princess was clearly in love with the marquis. So, after drinking five or six glasses of wine, His Majesty hemmed and hawed and then said, "You have only to say the word, Marquis, to become my son-in-law."

The marquis bowed and looked tenderly at the princess. That very day they were married. Puss, who had brought it all about, looked on mightily pleased. And ever afterward he lived in the castle as a great lord, and hunted mice for mere sport whenever he pleased.

The Cat on the Dovrefell

Once upon a time there was a man living up in Finmark who caught a big, white, furry bear, which he decided to take south as a present for the King of Denmark. It was Christmas Eve, and a heavy snow was falling as he crossed the Dovrefell. So he turned in at a cottage there and asked for lodging for himself, which he thought would be easy, and for his bear, which he guessed would be hard.

"Alas," said the man in the cottage, whose name was Halvor, "I have no lodging for you and your bear. In fact, I have none even for myself and my family. For every Christmas Eve a pack of trolls descends upon us, eating us out of house and home and sleeping in our beds into the bargain. Indeed, we have just decided to move out over the holidays, and not return till the house is free of them."

"Well, then," said the man with the bear, "you lose nothing by giving me the lodging I need. My bear can lie beside the stove yonder, and I can make do with the side room."

"So be it," agreed Halvor. "And if you will now muzzle your bear, who is breathing hard down my neck, I will proceed with arrangements for the guests."

Yes, that's how it was, for before the people of the house departed they had to put everything in order for the trolls. The

beds had to be made and the tables laid. Pools of porridge and mountains of sausage, masses of giblets and hashes of stew had to be set out for the trolls.

Soon the trolls were entering the house, some big, some little, some with two tails, and some with no tail at all, with noses like pokers or whiplashes, and ears like the handles of pitchers, looped, furled, and curled. They made themselves completely at home, stabbing fingers and snouts into sausages and almost washing themselves in the porridge.

Suddenly, one of the little trolls caught sight of the big white bear, who was lying beside the stove. He took a long sausage on a short fork and went and poked it against the bear's nose, screeching, "Pussycat, pussycat, will you have some sausage?"

"Grrr!" growled the white bear, and the sausage went flying through the air. "Grrr!" growled the white bear again, and the little troll followed it. "Grrr!" growled the white bear a third time, rising up and chasing the whole pack of them, as a cat chases mice, till they fled out of doors and vanished among the mountains.

On Christmas Eve next year, Halvor was at the edge of the forest cutting wood, when he heard a voice among the trees.

"Halvor! Halvor!" it cried.

"What do you want?" he asked.

"Have you that big cat with you still?"

"I have not, for she was taken south to the King of Denmark. But I have something else—her seven kittens, all bigger and fiercer than she."

"Thank you very much," shouted the troll in the wood. "That is all we wanted to know."

And from that day to this, the trolls have never again come to eat their Christmas dinner with Halvor on the Dovrefell.

The Wolf and the Seven Kids

There was once a goat who had seven little ones, and was as fond of them as ever mother was of her children. One day she had to go into the wood to fetch food for them, so she called them all round her.

"Dear children," said she, "I am going out into the wood. While I am gone, be on your guard against the wolf, for if he were to get inside he would eat you up, skin, bones, and all. The wretch often disguises himself, but he may always be known by his hoarse voice and black paws."

"Dear Mother," answered the kids, "you need not be afraid. We will take care of ourselves." And the mother bleated good-bye, and went on her way with an easy mind.

Not long afterward, someone came knocking at the door, crying, "Open the door, children. Your mother is back."

But the little kids knew it was the wolf by the hoarse voice. "We will not open the door," cried they, "for you are not our mother. She has a delicate and sweet voice, and your voice is hoarse. You must be the wolf."

Then off went the wolf to a shop, where he bought a big lump of chalk. He ate it to make his voice soft, and then he went back, knocked at the door, and cried, "Open the door, dear children. Your mother is here."

But the wolf had put his black paws against the window, and the kids, seeing this, cried out, "We will not open the door. Our mother has no black paws like you. You must be the wolf."

The wolf then ran to a baker. "Baker," said he, "I am hurt in the foot. Pray spread some dough over the place."

And when the baker had plastered his feet, he ran to the miller. "Miller," said he, "strew some white meal over my paws." But the miller refused, thinking the wolf must be up to no good. "If you don't do it," cried the wolf, "I'll eat you up." And the miller was afraid and did as he was told.

And then for the third time the rogue went to the door and knocked. "Open, children!" cried he. "Your dear mother has come home and brought you each something from the wood."

"First show us your paws," said the kids.

The wolf put his paws against the window, and when the kids saw that they were white, all seemed right, and they opened the door. But once he was inside they saw it was the wolf, and they were terrified and tried to hide themselves. The first crept under the table, the second jumped into the bed, the third climbed into the oven, the fourth ran into the kitchen, the fifth crawled into the cupboard, the sixth stooped under the sink, and the seventh squeezed into the clock case. But the wolf found and made short shrift of them. One after another he swallowed all but the youngest, who was well hidden in the clock case. And then the wolf, having gotten what he wanted, strolled forth into the green meadow, lay down under a tree, and fell fast asleep.

Soon afterward the mother goat came back from the wood. Oh, what a sight met her eyes! The door was standing wide open; table, chairs, and stools were all thrown about; dishes were broken; quilts and pillows were torn off the beds.

The mother goat sought her children, but they were nowhere to be found. She called to each of them by name, but nobody answered—until she called the name of the youngest.

"Here I am, Mother," a little voice cried, "in the clock case."

So she helped him out, and heard how the wolf had come and eaten all the rest. And you may think how she cried for the loss of her dear children. At last, in her grief she wandered out of doors, the youngest kid at her side.

When they came to the meadow, they saw the wolf lying under a tree, snoring so that the branches shook. The mother goat looked at him carefully. Suddenly, she noticed that something inside his body was moving and struggling. "Dear me," she thought. "Can it be that my poor children are still alive?"

The mother goat immediately sent the little kid back to the house for a pair of shears, a needle, and thread. Then she cut the wolf's body open. No sooner had she done so than one after another, the kids jumped out alive, for in his greediness the wolf had swallowed them whole. How happy they were!

"Now fetch some good hard stones," said the mother, "and we will fill his body with them as he lies asleep." And so the children fetched some in all haste, and put them inside the wolf, and the mother sewed him up quickly.

When the wolf at last awoke, the stones inside him made him feel very thirsty. As he was going to the brook to drink, they struck and rattled against each other. And so he cried out:

"What is this I feel inside me,
Knocking hard against my bones?
How should such a thing betide me!
They were kids, and now they're stones."

Soon the wolf reached the brook and stooped to drink. But the heavy stones weighed him down so that he fell over into the water and drowned. And when the seven little kids saw this, they cried out, "The wolf is dead, the wolf is dead!" And joining hands, they danced and danced with their mother.